PRIDE OF INDIA

VOLUME 3

ADAPTED FROM ORIGINAL
AMAR CHITRA KATHA COMICS

PRIDE OF INDIA

VOLUME 3

ADAPTED FROM ORIGINAL
Amar Chitra Katha Comics

WRITTEN BY
Pika Nani

TIMELESS
Amar Chitra Katha

RUPA

Published by
Rupa Publication India Pvt. Ltd.
7/ 16, Ansari Road, Daryaganj, New Delhi 110002

First published by Rupa Publication India Pvt. Ltd.
In collaboration with Amar Chitra Katha Pvt. Ltd. 2024

Sales centres:
Bengaluru, Chennai
Hyderabad, Jaipur, Kathmandu
Kolkata, Mumbai, Prayagraj

AMAR CHITRA KATHA PVT LTD
Office no. 5017/18/19/20
1AEROCITY NIBR Corporate Park
Andheri East, Sakinaka
Mumbai 400072

Art Director – Ketan Tondwalkar
Designed by Manoj Tandel

Adapted from the original ACK Comics
Original Illustrations
Lal Bahadur Shastri – Dilip Kadam
Rani Of Jhansi – Hema Joshi
Subhas Chandra Bose – H S Chavan & Sailo Chakravarty

P-ISBN: 978-93-6156-234-1
E-ISBN: 978-93-6156-120-7

First impression 2024

10 9 8 7 6 5 4 3 2 1

CONTENTS

RANI LAKSHMIBAI

Page No. 7

SUBHAS CHANDRA BOSE

Page No. 47

LAL BAHADUR SHASTRI

Page No. 89

Rani Lakshmibai

Her name alone invokes an image of a warrior woman charging her steed through enemy lines, sword raised for the attack! Rani Lakshmibai of Jhansi's story began at Varanasi. Her parents named her Manikarnika at birth. Little Manu, as her friends called her, was quite the tomboy. She had lost her mother at an early age and lived in the palace of the exiled Maratha ruler, Peshwa Bajirao II, at Bithur where her father was a courtier. Living within the walls of the palace, she played, studied, practiced sword fighting, and horseback riding, with the boys at the peshwa's court which included Rao Saheb, Nana Saheb, and Tatya Tope.

Manu loved to read and write, and was more independent than most girls her age.

Years passed and Manu turned eleven. As was the custom in those days, her relatives wanted to get her married off. "It's time you found a husband for Manu," they told her father.

"The astrologers have foretold a royal match for her," her father replied with pride. And the prophecy came true. A year later Manu was to marry Gangadhar Rao, the Maharaja of Jhansi. Manikarnika was to be re-named Lakshmibai in honour of the goddess of wealth and victory.

In May 1842, the wedding was celebrated with great pomp and ceremony. The king arrived in a golden howdah, on the back of a royal elephant. The wedding procession was accompanied by the beating of drums and the fanfare of trumpets. Cannons boomed in salute. The people of Jhansi welcomed their new queen with great joy.

In 1851, Rani Lakshmibai gave birth to a son. The birth of the prince was a joyous occasion for the people of Jhansi. But three months later the child died. The whole kingdom was plunged into grief, along with the parents.

The maharaja was already old and frail. He had another thing worrying him. "Alas! I have no son to succeed me. What shall I do?" He was very ill and knew he had little time left.

According to the royal customs, a king without a natural heir could adopt a child and name him or her as their heir. The maharaja took a decision to adopt a son.

The adoption took place on November 19, 1853. Once again there was an air of celebration in the kingdom. Rani

Lakshmibai and the Maharaja were happy parents to the little boy they named Damodar Rao. British officers were invited to the court as well to make sure they were aware of the adoption of an heir to Jhansi. The Maharaja's wish was that Rani Lakshmibai should rule Jhansi until the boy came of age.

A day later, the Maharaja died.

Rani Lakshmibai, still a teenager, took over the reins of the kingdom. "The fate of the people of Jhansi is now in my hands! I will not let them down!" she vowed to herself.

Rani Lakshmibai devoted herself to the efficient administration of her state. She was a quick learner. Her first action upon taking over the rule of the kingdom was to send a petition to the British Governor General for the recognition of her adopted son as the future king of Jhansi. She would hold durbars and hear the grievances of her subjects and settle their disputes. She was a kind ruler. "There was a drought last year. We should lower the tax on wheat," she told her minister.

One day, two men in red and gold uniforms of the British army arrived in her court.

"The British Government has decided to take the state of Jhansi under its wings," one of the men read out the message sent by the Governor General Dalhousie. The man went on to quote the Doctrine of Lapse. The system allowed the British to assume control of states whose rulers died without a natural heir. This was just a pretext to annex more land under the British rule.

The young queen boiled with rage. "I will not give up my Jhansi!" she proclaimed.

The news about the impending British takeover spread among the subjects. It was a day of mourning in Jhansi. Rani Lakshmibai

had won over the people's confidence with her intelligence, kindness and execution of justice. They wanted their queen to rule the kingdom and not some foreign government. The complete support of her people renewed Lakshmibai's spirits. She came to a decision. "The Rani of Jhansi was not born to weep! I will send an envoy to London with an appeal."

She was able to put her arguments in a strongly-worded letter. But the envoy returned with bad news. "The British government has rejected your appeal!"

Lakshmibai was furious. "They have no sense of justice. I will not obey them!"

When the British forces came, she had to move out of her fort. But the enormity of British power and presence could not break Rani Lakshmibai's spirit.

All over India, the British were becoming more and more ruthless. They annexed Satara, a town in Maharashtra, without any justification. The ancient handloom industry in Satara was tainted with cheap British clothes. Many such factors led to the revolt of 1857, but the main factor was the introduction of greased cartridges by the East India Company. The sepoys had to bite the cartridge of the new rifle with their teeth. This was unacceptable to the Indian soldiers as the cartridges were believed to have been greased with the fat of beef and pork. Shocked at the Britishers' attempt to taint their religion, the Indian soldiers joined hands in the collective mutiny.

On May 10, 1857, the Indian rebellion started in Meerut. The Indian soldiers of the barracks of Meerut openly revolted, shooting their British officers and releasing imprisoned comrades. Then they marched on Delhi where they received a warm welcome by the people. The aged ex-emperor Bahadur Shah Zafar was reinstated on the Mughal throne, and Delhi became the headquarters of the nationalist soldiers. The seizure of Delhi set the model for the whole mutiny, which then spread throughout northern India. Thousands of soldiers turned against their officers.

The people on the streets of Jhansi had only one topic to discuss.

"Did you hear? The nationalist soldiers have seized Lucknow!" said a bullock cart driver.

"And Sitapur too," said a woman selling vegetables.

"Kanpur as well," added an old man.

Now they are marching on Jhansi!" said a young man on horseback.

The British officers in Jhansi too had heard about the advancing nationalist soldiers. They ran to Lakshmibai and begged for help. "We want you to take over the kingdom until the British authority is re-established," they pleaded.

"You refused to give me my kingdom when I asked for it. Now that you cannot keep it, you are handing it to me! The Indian troops will destroy me if I give you protection. You had better save your lives as best as you can," was her reply.

The British were powerless against the nationalist soldiers and they knew that.

The nationalist leaders decided to let Lakshmibai rule Jhansi and proceeded towards Delhi. They knew the British had treated her unfairly as well. But Lakshmibai did not want to take this position for granted. She wanted to know if the people of her kingdom wanted her or preferred the British rule. She called a conference in court the next day. "I want my people to decide who should rule Jhansi," she announced.

The members of the court had a long discussion. A large crowd was anxiously waiting outside for the decision of their representatives. Finally emerging from the balcony, the minister announced, "Rani Lakshmibai will take the throne, and Jhansi will be independent."

The people were ecstatic. Chants of "Long live Rani Lakshmibai!" echoed in the air.

Thus, Lakshmibai resumed control of her state. It was a period of peace and calm for Jhansi. Lakshmibai took great interest in the welfare of her subjects. She was a great patroness of art and literature and welcomed performers and artisans from all over India to her court. The state

library was her special interest. She often bought new books, including expensive ones, and expanded the library.

The first to challenge Lakshmibai's rule was Sadashiv Rao. He was a distant nephew of the late Maharaja. One day, he turned up in the main bazaar and announced pompously "I am the king of Jhansi!" But that did not impress the people. "Rani Lakshmibai is our queen!" they declared and shooed him away.

Rani Lakshmibai heard about Sadashiv Rao's claims and sent her troops after him. He was defeated in a single encounter.

A little while later, the princes of Datia and Orcha, two neighbouring states, plotted to take Jhansi from Lakshmibai. Their intention was to divide Jhansi amongst themselves. They thought the queen, being a woman, would be weak and they decided to send a battalion of their soldiers to attack the

fort. The guards spotted the approaching army and sent for their queen. Adept in military planning, Lakshmibai said, "We must not waste men needlessly. We will only attack when they are near."

The enemy soldiers were happy to see no firing from the fort. They thought they could storm the fort and occupy it.

Boom! Boom! Balls of fire began to rain on the enemy. Lakshmibai's troop had begun their attack. And since the other soldiers were so close, they could easily target them with their arms and ammunitions.

The enemy retreated in confusion. Lakshmibai's strategy had worked.

But that night, Orcha's troops got their big guns out, and under the cover of darkness attacked Jhansi's forces again. The Jhansi army was taken by surprise and suffered losses. They were ready to give up. Lakshmibai heard their loud cries of despair and appeared on horseback. "Don't lose courage. Jhansi never admits defeat!" she said brandishing a sword in her hand. Seeing their queen ready to fight with them, the troops were filled with courage and demolished the enemy on the battlefield.

The next day Rani Lakshmibai held a grand durbar to celebrate the victory. She honoured all her soldiers for their bravery in the war.

However, there was bad news from the north. The British had captured Delhi. The emperor's sons were treacherously shot and the emperor was imprisoned.

Nana Saheb, Lakshmibai's childhood friend and the peshwa of the Maratha empire had been one of the leaders of the 1857 rebellion. The British garrison in Kanpur had been forced to surrender to him. News reached that the British had reoccupied Kanpur by defeating Nana Saheb's army. Oudh, a princely state in the Awadh region, had also been conquered. There was a looming fear that it would be Jhansi's turn next.

Not one to sit idle, Lakshmibai began preparations to face an attack from the British.

She assessed her army and realised they needed more soldiers as well as a fire-brigade. She examined the armoury, where swords, guns, and ammunitions were stocked and procured. She also made sure there was enough food for the people and fodder for the livestock in case of a long siege.

One day, Rani Lakshmibai left her fort alone on foot and reached the main street. It was buzzing with people going about their daily chores. A group of people noticed their queen and stopped to pay their respects. Soon the word spread and a crowd had gathered around her. Lakshmibai smiled at her people. She was here on an important mission: to enlist soldiers for her army. "How many of you will fight for your Jhansi?" she shouted pumping her fist in the air.

"I will," said a man. Many men put up their hands.

"We all will," said a youth.

Lakshmibai noticed that the group of women were silent. Turning towards them she said, "The women of Jhansi must help too!"

The women were surprised. There were murmurings from the group. "What can we do?" said a voice from the crowd.

"I'm a woman too. If I can fight for my country, so can you!" said Lakshmibai.

She was the perfect role model to the women of her kingdom. Inspired by her, women enlisted as troopers and gunners and were taught to ride, shoot and fence. Lakshmibai herself took an interest in their training. Later on, the women took on watch duties and cared for the wounded.

Jhansi was ready to face a military attack. But the tension was taking a toll on its citizens.

Rani Lakshmibai was aware of this and wanted to do something to inspire confidence among her people. She came up with a unique idea. All the women of Jhansi were invited to a Haldi Kumkum ceremony. The palace was decked up in flower garlands and oil lamps. Dressed in colourful silk sarees, and dazzling jewellery, the women applied Halid Kumkum to each other. The Rani gave them gifts and treated everyone to delicious food. The women were bowled over by her generosity. They went back home and shared the joy with their families. The people were convinced that with a ruler like her, Jhansi would always be victorious and independent.

Meanwhile the British were advancing rapidly. They had turned their attention to north-central India and captured Sehore and Rahatgarh. They took Sagar and defeated the

Raja of Banpur, an ally of Jhansi. They would be at the gates of Jhansi within a few weeks.

"Why don't you ask your old friends Tatya Tope and Rao Saheb for help?" the palace ministers advised Rani Lakshmibai.

Lakshmibai had already thought about it and had reached out to them. "I have. Tatya Tope has attacked the Rajas of Panna and Charkhari, staunch allies of the British."

"But the British are still determined to attack Jhansi," said a courtier.

Jhansi's political importance made it a prime target.

Rani Lakshmibai being a democratic ruler cared for her subject's opinions. She did not want to force a war on them. She called a representative meeting of her people. "I think we should fight. But I leave the decision to your hands," she told them.

A few were of the opinion that they should save their homes and not go to war. But the majority were in favour of fighting. "We will uphold the independence of Jhansi. No foreigner will rule over us," they vowed.

Rani Lakshmibai was overjoyed. "You have taken a brave and noble decision. We will fight. If victorious we will enjoy the freedom. If defeated or slain we earn eternal glory."

The crowd broke out in chants of praise. "Long live Rani Lakshmibai!", "Victory to our queen!"

The queen then issued a proclamation that the military should be on high alert and ready to strike.

On the dawn of March 25, 1858, British guns began to bombard Jhansi. Rani Lakshmibai and her army were positioned in the fort. Lakshmibai's gunners answered every shot with return fire. The queen raced up and down the ramparts of the fort, shouting encouragement to her men.

For five days the British guns pounded day and night but with little result. Then a parapet and tower of the fort were slightly damaged. The troops rushed to

repair the breach. In the distance they saw a welcome sight. Tatya Tope was coming to the rescue with his army. The soldiers could see an enormous bonfire lit in the distance. They were sure that the British would be defeated now.

But the British were not about to give up. They brought two heavy duty cannons and bombarded Tatya's men. The next day, in a single encounter they defeated his army.

The news reached Lakshmibai. She gathered her officers. They were losing their willpower. She had to reignite the fire in their belly. "We must not lose heart. We can fight the British alone. You have fought with matching courage before. I am depending on you. I know you can do it!"

"We will fight to the last man," said a soldier.

"Victory will be ours!" cried the troops.

On April 3, at midnight, the British troops silently made their way to the damaged tower with a ladder.

"Look, that's where we should climb," whispered a British officer.

"Our ally in the queen's camp has kept his word," said another.

"Of course, he was paid well," retorted the first.

The British had bribed a man in the queen's camp to be their spy. He had given them information about the damaged part of the fort walls, through which they could enter. The Jhansi army could defend against an external enemy but it was not prepared for betrayal by one of its own.

As the British invaded the fort, the soldiers gave a tough fight. Swords clashed, guns blazed and the battle raged on. An attendant quickly woke Lakshmibai from her sleep. The queen watched the attacked tower through her binoculars. The British contingent had entered her fort and her soldiers were putting up a determined fight, but they would soon be outnumbered. She realised the chances of victory were slim, but she was not ready to surrender.

With a shield and a sword in hand, she mounted her horse. Leading her troops from the front, she charged at the British with all her might. The counter-attack was so unexpected and fierce that the British were forced to take cover for a while. But the battle was far from over.

Lakshmibai told her generals, "I have decided not to surrender. Those who want to die may remain with me, others may leave the fort."

The ministers convinced her to leave the fort and continue the fight with the help of their ally, Rao Saheb at Kalpi.

At midnight, with her young child tied to her back, the queen and her guards left the fort on horseback. They had to

move silently to avoid being captured by the enemy. It was a huge risk, but for Lakshmibai it was the only option.

The British soldiers were shocked when they found out that the queen had escaped.

"Let us give her a chase!" they cried.

"She has killed two soldiers who tried to capture her!" replied an officer.

Instead, the British went on to wreak havoc in Jhansi. They even destroyed the state library. They wanted to teach the city a lesson so that no one would dare challenge them again.

After a long and tiring journey, Lakshmibai rode into Kalpi and its formidable fort. She was welcomed by Rao Saheb, her childhood friend. "Welcome brave warrior. I need your support in my struggle."

"Nothing will give me greater happiness than to die on the battlefield serving under the Maratha flag," said Lakshmibai.

Rao Saheb knew about Lakshmibai's capabilities as a warrior. He asked her to inspect the troops. After her inspection she gave her valuable input to have better discipline among the soldiers, she recommended military drills and exercises every morning.

In a few days, news reached the camp that the British were planning a siege on Kalpi.

"Let's go out and meet them at Koonch," suggested Lakshmibai.

"That's a good idea. We will face them in the open," said Rao Saheb.

"But, we must have a strong rear-guard," advised Lakshmibai who had experience of the British army's tactics of attacking from the least expected side.

"We are all veterans in the art of war! Let the British come," replied Rao Saheb.

The overconfident nationalist leader did not listen to her counsel about having a strong rear-guard. During the battle, a contingent of the British army attacked from the back, and Rao Saheb's army was forced to flee. He was ready to surrender, but Lakshmibai stopped him. "Look! The nawab of Banda, an ally, has just arrived with a force of two thousand cavalry, guns and infantry."

An emergency council of war was held to consider their next move.

"Our situation is getting worse every hour. What should we do?" asked Rao Sahib.

"We should fight to the end. We can still retrieve our honour if we offer a determined resistance and the troops observe discipline," said Lakshmibai.

But the clever strategy of the British again won the day and Rao Saheb's army fled in confusion.

Rani Lakshmibai could not stand aside and watch the defeat. She mounted her horse and charged at the enemy like a tigress. "Victory will be ours!" she roared.

Her bravery encouraged the other leaders to join the attack. The enemy retreated. But then Sir Hugh Rose, the British General ordered the camel corps to charge. The Peshwa's men, who were on horses, were unable to withstand the attack and fell back in disarray.

The revolutionary spirit was completely shattered. The British took over the fort of Kalpi on May 26, 1858.

The rebel leaders, Rao Saheb, Tatya Tope, Nawab of Banda and of course Rani Lakshmibai had escaped capture. They held another urgent meeting.

"How about we harass the enemy by guerrilla warfare?" suggested the Nawab.

"That's an excellent plan," Rao Saheb agreed.

"That was possible for the Marathas because they possessed unconquerable fortresses. We cannot fight without a strong fort," said Lakshmibai. "I think we should march to Gwalior and obtain the help of the maharaja. With that fort in our hands, we can still carry on the war and win."

Like Jhansi, Gwalior was strategically significant. The Gwalior Fort was set atop steep rocks, rising above the surrounding planes. It was considered impregnable.

"I agree," said the Nawab. "Though the Maharaja is an ally of the British, his people are on our side."

They sent him a message but instead of helping with money or supplies, he ordered his troops to attack the rebels. But by now everyone in India had heard about Rani Lakshmibai and her brave fight with the Britishers. So, when the rebel leaders, headed by Lakshmibai rode into the city, it was enough to make the Gwalior army drop their weapons. The rebel forces occupied Gwalior without any opposition.

Rao Saheb held a grand durbar to proclaim the leadership of the Maratha Confederacy. A huge feast was held, the sound of trumpets and chanting of prayers rang through the fort walls.

"Rao Saheb has saved the honour of our country," said a courtier as cries of "Long live the Peshwa!" rang out.

As the ceremonies continued, Lakshmibai grew impatient. She was concerned about Rose's army's next move. "We have funds and a well-equipped army. We should prepare for the next struggle," she warned the others. But the rebel leaders did not listen to her. They were under the delusion that there was plenty of time to prepare for the next attack.

As Lakshmibai had feared, very soon, General Rose's forces marched on Gwalior. Rao Saheb was totally unprepared and didn't know what to do.

Take your troops out for one last glorious attack. I am ready to do my duty, you do yours! God be with you!" Lakshmibai told him.

Then, wrapping a red turban around her head, she got dressed in battle gear. Taking a deep breath, she mounted her horse.

Lakshmibai drew her sword out from its sheath and held it aloft, as she galloped towards the battlefield. Just the sight of the approaching warrior queen made the enemy nervous. She broke into the enemy lines with her sword slashing at the enemy troops. A fierce battle ensued.

In a little while, a voice from her army cried out. "British reinforcements have arrived! All is lost!"

"I will not lose hope. I will never surrender," said a fiery Lakshmibai. She charged at the British, slaying them left and right. The enemy attacked and injured her, but she carried on fighting until she was fatally wounded.

A few of her soldiers saw their wounded queen and carried her out of the battlefield.

Even in the face of death she was courageous. "Carry on the glorious fight, my brave soldiers. The days of freedom shall soon dawn," she said and breathed her last breath. Thus, ended the life of the young warrior queen.

The 1857 War of Independence marked the beginning of an active and united national movement, which sowed the seeds of independence for India.

Rani Lakshmibai's story of courage has become a legend and has been immortalised in various songs, ballads, paintings and folklore. She became an inspiration to freedom fighters who came after her. Subhas Chandra Bose named his women's regiment as the Jhansi Rani regiment. She is considered India's greatest female hero in the struggle for freedom.

Subhas Chandra Bose

It was break time at school. Children ran about the playground, shouting and laughing. A group of them were kicking a football around and creating a ruckus. Unaffected by his surroundings, a little boy, wearing a crisp white shirt and blue shorts sat under a tree, completely immersed in a book.

"Who is that boy?" asked a new teacher to her colleague.

"That is Subhas, our favourite student," came the reply.

Netaji Subhas Chandra Bose was born in Cuttack, Odisha on January 23, 1897. His father, Janaki Nath Bose, was a well-known lawyer. His mother, Prabhavati, was a religious woman and the anchor of the family.

When he was five Subhas was admitted to the

Protestant European School in Cuttack, where his elder brothers studied as well. He gained proficiency in English as it was the medium of instruction. But soon the Bengali language was made compulsory for Bengalis at the matric level. Since no Indian languages were taught at his existing school, Subhas who was twelve by then, was transferred to the Ravenshaw Collegiate School.

The first day of the new school, was a bit of a culture shock for Subhas. He stood out in his old uniform — a white shirt, shorts and a tie, while the other students were dressed in dhoti and kurta. Subhas wanted to fit in with his new classmates. The next day, he too wore a dhoti and a white kurta. His father noticed him leaving for school. "What is the matter? Why are you dressed like this?" he asked.

"This is how they dress at the new school, father," replied Subhas.

It wasn't just the dress that was Indian. The ideals and principals of the school were deeply rooted in Indian-ness. The headmaster Beni Madhav Das was a true nationalist. He would often tell his students, "Never forget, we are Indians, and India is a great country. While you learn your lessons, learn to love your country too."

Subhas's mind absorbed the ideals of patriotism at a young age.

A few months later, it was the eve of the first anniversary of the martyrdom of Khudiram Bose, a young Indian revolutionary who fought the British and laid down his life for the country. Subhas wanted to pay tribute to the martyred hero. He discussed with his classmates. "We have to do something special to mark the occasion. Why don't we fast tomorrow in his memory?" The other students agreed at once.

Beni Madhav Das was proud of his students. He too fasted with them. But the British did not take his anti-government stancekindly, and transferred him to Bengal.

Subhas, along with the other students, went to the railway station to see him off. The headmaster was well aware of his student's potential. When Subhas touched his feet, he

blessed him, "You are destined to be great, Subhas. May God bless you."

The next day, Subhas hung a photograph of Beni Madhav Das in the school hall. He told all the students, "We must never forget what our guru taught us. We must live up to all that he stands for."

And they did not forget. When a small pox epidemic hit a village, unafraid of being infected with the disease, Subhas formed a volunteer corps with his classmates to nurse the poor and neglected patients.

Subhas was exceptionally good in his studies. The days flew by and he passed his matriculation exam and stood second in the university. He had continued his practice of wearing a white dhoti and kurta. By now he also wore spectacles. His love for reading had continued from childhood. He was inspired by the works of Swami Vivekananda where he found answers to many of the questions arising in his mind. He even began practicing yoga. But he was still restless. He felt the need of a guru who would show him the right path. He made plans with a like-minded friend to go in search of a guru. Together they visited many pilgrim centres hoping to find a true guide. But his search proved futile, as all the holy men he met were more interested

in money and other worldly matters than in spiritualism. Disillusioned, he returned home.

"Subhas you can still pursue your ideal. You may have to do it without a spiritual guide," said his father who had been worried sick about him.

"I have realised that father," sighed Subhas.

Subhas secured admission to the Presidency college in Calcutta (Kolkata). He was a good student, but right from the start, he was aware of the rude behaviour of the British teachers towards Indian students. The worst of them was Professor Oten. Once, during a college meeting, Oten burst out, "You are all barbarians! It is we English who have civilised you."

This was the last straw. The students couldn't take the humiliation anymore. They were seething with rage. Subhas, being a natural leader was the one to bring all his classmates together to address the issue. "We have tolerated enough. We must protest," he suggested.

A batch of students, led by him marched to the principal, Mr James's office. "Sir, Professor Oten's behaviour towards us is rude and unjustified. Please ask him to stop."

The principal, an Englishman, sided with the professor. "How dare you criticise your teacher," he told the motley delegation. "Go and beg his forgiveness."

The students were shocked by this injustice. They were at a loss about what to do. The next day Subhas stood outside the gates of the college and spoke to the students. "We demand better treatment. Boycott all classes!" Such was his charisma that over a thousand students participated in the strike. None of the classes could be held. The strike went on for three days. The Indian teachers also supported them. This is considered to be the first strike in modern India.

At last Professor Oten apologised and the strike was called off. But Oten never forgave the boys. One day, he hit a student for a trivial reason, "Can't you walk without flapping your slippers."

The student community was furious. A few of them laid in wait as the professor left for home in the evening and attacked him from behind.

Since Subhas was considered to be the student leader, he was summoned to the principal's office the next day. "Bose, we are not sure if you attacked the professor yourself, but we think you were involved. We cannot tolerate this crime. You are rusticated from the college."

Subhas did not argue and returned to his home in Cuttack. His only consolation was that his parents believed in him and stood by his side.

Soon Durga Puja arrived. It was celebrated with great splendour and religious fervour all over Bengal. Not one to sit brooding over the past, Subhas decided to organise a public Durga puja with his friends. They fed the poor and formed a 'nursing brotherhood' to serve neglected patients. His initiatives for the community soon made him a popular figure.

People were impressed by his intelligence and hardworking nature. They urged him to go back to college. Subhas too felt it was time to continue his education. He approached Dr Asutosh Mukherji, vice chancellor of Calcutta University. He was helpful in ensuring that Subhas got another chance. After persistent efforts, he gained admission to the Scottish Church College.

At college, he joined the university training crops. This was the first time he donned the military uniform. He hoped the military training would be useful later when he would fight the British.

The commanding officer of the division was Captain Grey, an Englishman. At that time, Professor Oten was the director of public instruction in Bengal. He came to visit the training camp one day.

Subhas was worried when he saw his old professor. "Will he take revenge on me, get me removed from here as well?"

Oten was watching the parade. "The Indian boys are as good as the English boys," he remarked. Suddenly his eyes fell on Subhas. He looked smart marching in his khaki uniform. Oten pointed him out and asked Captain Grey, "That boy, is he any good?"

"Bose? He's one of the best," replied the captain without any hesitation.

Later, Oten approached his old student. "Bose, your captain speaks highly of you. I want to offer you a non-commissioned post in the corps."

"Thank you, sir. It's a great honour. I'm grateful to you," said a surprised Subhas.

Subhas graduated from Calcutta University at the age of twenty-two. He went to England to appear for the Indian Civil Service examination. It was a tough exam with very few vacancies, yet he managed to stand fourth.

His friends went to meet him.

"Congratulations, Subhas, you have a bright future ahead of you."

"Thank you, but I plan to resign from the service," said Subhas coolly.

"What? Why?" asked his friends in shock.

"I appeared for my Indian Civil Service exams to educate myself, not to become a part of the administrative machine of the British Empire," said Subhas. His resignation created a sensation in England and India.

Subhas set sail for India. He was very clear in his mind about his goal in life—to work towards liberating the country from British rule. Immediately after landing in Bombay, he went to meet Mahatma Gandhi, with a plan to join him in the freedom struggle. But they differed on the question of approach - Gandhi's road to freedom was a non-violent one. Subhas believed all means were acceptable to achieve independence.

Gandhiji suggested that Subhas should work with Deshbandhu Chittaranjan Das, a influential leader in Bengal. Subhas travelled to Calcutta to meet him.

Deshbandu welcomed him and his ideas warmly. Subhas felt he had finally found

his guru. This was Subhas's first step in national politics. He was a fast learner and soon became Das's right-hand man and an active worker of the party. In order to earn a living, he took on the post of principal of the National College at Calcutta.

On December 10, 1921, he was arrested for the first time for anti-government activities and sentenced to six months of imprisonment. Subhas laughed at the judgement. "A mere six months! I'm no common thief."

Chittaranjan Das soon had differences with other leaders of the Congress. He held a meeting with Subash and others. "I have decided to form a new party. Our Swaraj Party will work within Congress."

In the Calcutta Corporation elections held in 1924, the Swaraj party bagged almost all the seats. The public was jubilant and took out processions to celebrate the victory.

Das was elected mayor and Subhas was appointed the chief executive officer (C.E.O) of the Calcutta Corporation.

The Swarajists introduced many changes in the administration. Khadi was made the official dress for the corporation workers. Subhas as the C.E.O., personally inspected the work of the municipal staff on the streets. He formed a volunteer corps to sell khadi and do other social and political work. The British were uneasy with the rising popularity of Subhas and declared the corps illegal. All meetings, demonstrations and processions were banned.

Subhas was furious with this decision. He started sending five volunteers every day to demonstrate against the British injustice. Calcutta was already very tense. To add to it, one day a European was murdered. The government made a false charge of masterminding the murder on Subhas and arrested him again.

The public did not take the arrest lying down. They demonstrated outside the jail and took out rallies. "Free Subhas Bose immediately! Subhas Bose zindabad!" could be heard on every street. Frightened by the mood of the public, the British government sent Subhas to Mandalay jail in Burma.

"I am being punished without even a trial. For a crime I did not even commit. This is injustice," thought Subhas as he slept on the cold stone floor of the jail, shivering from head to toe.

The jail was horrible. There was no shelter from the lashing rains or the sweltering heat. It was more like a cage for beasts than a prison

for men. Under the inhuman and unhealthy conditions, Subhas contracted tuberculosis. He grew very ill. The news spread in Calcutta like wildfire. People took to the streets to demand his release.

The British government put a condition. The jailer read it out to Subhas. "The government has agreed to release you on the condition that you will leave for Europe immediately."

Subhas was very weak physically, but mentally he was as strong as ever. "I refuse conditional freedom. I would rather die here."

His health worsened to an alarming level and the government had to release him unconditionally. After his release he spent some time recovering his health at Dalhousie, a charming hill station in Himachal. By then Chittaranjan Das had passed away and Subhas vowed to carry forward the freedom struggle, the way his guru had done.

In 1928, the Indian National Congress held a session in Calcutta. Subhas organised a volunteer corps, a band of young men dressed in smart military uniforms, and he himself took on the role of its General Officer Commanding. Even after the session was over the corps continued their activities. The government suspected the corps of working against the British Government and arrested him.

While Subhas was in jail he was elected as the mayor of Calcutta Corporation in 1931. There were fresh protests leading to his release. Subhas took up his duties as the mayor of Calcutta. January 26 was declared as a day of taking oath for the independence of the country. He planned public meetings and a rally to hoist the Indian flag. The government quickly issued a notice – processions and meetings were banned and illegal.

Undeterred, Subhas proudly held aloft the Indian flag and led a procession from the corporation building. But the police arrived and carried out a lathi charge against them, hitting everyone mercilessly with sticks.

They arrested Subhas and put him in jail at Insin near Rangoon. Once again, he fell ill and his condition deteriorated. This time not just the people in Calcutta, but his supporters all over India protested for his release.

On his release, he travelled to Europe for treatment. His health gradually improved in Vienna. He went on to tour many European countries to promote the cause of Indian freedom. He met many Indian students and European politicians. He was turning into an experienced statesman, with his ability to deal with world leaders and important public issues.

While he was abroad, he heard that his father was on his deathbed in Calcutta.

He rushed to Bombay without the government's permission. But he was in for a rude shock. The police accosted him, "Mr Bose, you are arrested for violating the government's order."

"But my father is dying. I want to be near him," said Subhas.

But his pleas fell on deaf ears. His father died before he could reach Calcutta. A bitter Subhas went back to Europe.

He was finally allowed to return to India in 1938, when he was elected Congress president at the Haripur session. He looked dapper in a medallion-style tie and a shawl wrapped around him from one shoulder. In his victory speech, in front of all the Congress leaders and party-men he urged for action, "War in Europe is imminent. This is our chance to strike at the British. The country is ready to fight."

The other leaders of the party, including Gandhiji did not agree with him. They opposed his re-election for the next session at Tripura the following year, but Subhas Chandra Bose had a good amount of support and won easily. But worried that his differences with Mahatma Gandhi would split the party, he resigned.

Within three days, he formed the Forward Bloc within the Congress party with his supporters. "We demand Indian independence here and now!" he declared passionately.

They made plans to agitate for the removal of the Holwell monument in Calcutta, which was considered to be a symbol of India's slavery. Subhas was arrested and sent to jail. He was convinced by now that only an armed struggle could save India. He resolved to set out and seek the help of other foreign nations. But first he had to get out of jail. And so, began an elaborate plan for what is known today as his 'great escape'.

He began a fast in jail refusing to eat or drink anything. "You must release me or I will fast unto death," he warned the officers.

Afraid of public anger if anything were to happen to Subhas, the government released him. But they kept his house under surveillance and his every movement was monitored. But Subhas was already putting the next part of his plan into action. He kept a low profile and grew a beard. At midnight, on January 17, 1941, a bearded Muslim dressed

in a long coat and broad pyjamas exited the house in a chauffeured car. The guards did not realise that he was Subhas Bose!

He reached the railway station and got into a train. He had managed to fool the guards, but he had a long journey ahead of him. Not wanting to raise any suspicions while talking to his co-passengers, he assumed the identity of Moulvi Jiauddin, an insurance agent. He journeyed to Peshawar, but there was a problem. He could not speak a word of the Pashto language. There was a danger of him being identified by the Pashto speaking spies working for the British. But where there is a problem, there is a solution. Subhas pretended to be a deaf and dumb Pathan, a clever disguise that would not arouse suspicion. He was accompanied by another Indian who was also in disguise.

Subhas reached Kabul in a loaded truck posing as a road construction worker. He crossed the border to Moscow and finally

reached Berlin. His broadcast from the Azad Hind radio in Germany sent shock waves among the British and invigorated the Indian masses. He organised a small army with Indian prisoners of war, who had previously fought for the British. The soldiers stood in their khaki uniforms as Subhas addressed them. "Our well-trained army will fight the British. We will win freedom for India!"

He even met Hitler and sought his help, but he soon realised that Germany was too far off to wage war against the British in India. He set his sights on Japan. They had grown into a world power by occupying key colonies in Asia.

A few days later, somewhere in the middle of the Indian Ocean, on the roof of the German submarine U-180, stood a solitary man. The wind lashed his face and threatened to throw him off. A small rubber lifeboat bobbed on the waves nearby. It looked like at any moment the boat could overturn and be swallowed up by the choppy ocean. The man got onto the lifeboat and clung to the ropes with all his strength as it moved forward. Slowly, like a whale emerging from the sea, another huge submarine surfaced. The figure slowly climbed aboard the Japanese submarine. The brave man was none other than Subhas Chandra Bose!

This was the only civilian transfer between two submarines of two different navies in World War II. Bose had managed the impossible with his determination. This dangerous trip was undertaken by him to reach Japan and get them on his side.

After many months of navigating the turbulent sea, he reached Tokyo on June 13, 1943. From there he travelled to Singapore where he was received by Rash Behari Bose and other revolutionaries fighting the British Empire from outside India.

Subhas Chandra Bose raised an army with Indian prisoners of war captured by the Japanese. He adopted a military uniform of khaki pants, shirt and a Gandhi topi. He motivated the soldiers with his speech. "You were fighting for an alien power. Now you shall fight for your own country."

The soldiers called him 'Netaji'—a leader who guides them on the right path—out of respect.

He also formed the Rani of Jhansi regiment with Indian girls, which was the first of its kind in Asia.

On October 21, 1943, he announced the formation of the Azad Hind government. It gave Indian people the first experience of independent statehood after two centuries of being enslaved by British rule.

After pondering about the various types of

greetings in India like 'namaste' and 'aadab', he decided on 'Jai Hind' as their official salutation. Bose had always been a powerful orator. He knew how to rouse the public emotions. In a rally he declared, "Give me your blood, I promise you freedom."

The crowd was infused with energy and cried out, "Netaji zindabad! Netaji zindabad!"

He was a popular leader and got massive support from the Indian community in Southeast Asia. They donated generously to the cause and enlisted with the I.N.A. in hordes.

The I.N.A.'s first action was in the Eastern Indian frontiers. Subhas Chandra Bose directed his army to march to the battlefield.

"Chalo Delhi!" he proclaimed. "We may die, but our country shall be free!"

The army made its way via Rangoon to Kohima. It was a long and treacherous journey through forests, streams and hills. They strategically cut off the Imphal - Kohima Road on March 14, 1944. Imphal was completely surrounded by the I.N.A. and the Japanese. Subhas and his army entered Kohima four days later. There was a sense of pride as the tricolour flag was raised for the first time in the town. But the good fortune did not last long. The British and their allies were not ready to give up and stayed entrenched in town. After several months of fighting in Imphal, the Japanese faced heavy losses and were forced to retreat.

The I.N.A. got a message from the Japanese. "We can't give you air support. It is vitally needed in the Pacific."

This was a big blow to the Indian soldiers on the ground, who depended on Japan for arms and food. The situation looked bleak, but the worst was yet to come.

The sky darkened and thunder clouds began to rumble. Lightning flashed across the sky. Raindrops began to fall, fast and furious, like bullets attacking the soldiers from above.

The already troubled I.N.A. had no other option but to retreat.

The mood was serious and there was a sense of despair. Subhas Chandra Bose's dedication

to the cause of freedom had not waivered, but he realised he needed to motivate and inspire his followers. In a landmark broadcast to his soldiers and countrymen on April 24, he said, "Comrades! At this critical hour I have only one word for you and that is, if you have to go down temporarily then go down fighting with the tricolour held aloft. Go down as heroes, upholding the highest code of honour and discipline. I have always said that the darkest hour precedes dawn. India shall be free."

The Japanese surrendered to the British-American forces. Without the Japanese support, the I.N.A. also surrendered on August 16, 1945.

Subhas Chandra Bose and a small number of troops did not surrender and escaped capture. But the British-American forces were putting all their efforts into tracking Bose. It was clear that his life was in danger.

The soldiers of I.N.A. pleaded with him. "Netaji, please leave for a safe place. It's too risky for you here."

"War is a risky business. Didn't you know?" joked Bose. He had no intention of leaving.

"But we need you safe, to lead us again," the soldiers pleaded. "We cannot allow you to be caught by the British."

Bose thought about it for some time and came to a resolve. "I will not give up. I want to start again from some other place."

On August 17, Netaji boarded a Japanese plane for an unknown destination. The plane was said to have crashed, causing Netaji's death. But many of his followers refused to acknowledge it and believed he was alive somewhere in hiding. The mystery surrounding his death remains unsolved to this day.

Netaji Subhas Chandra Bose was one of the most charismatic and brave freedom fighters of India. He created a mass awakening and inspired thousands to join the struggle for Independence. His life story continues to inspire future generations.

Lal Bahadur Shastri

The year was 1905. The main bazaar at Prayag, an ancient town in Uttar Pradesh, was buzzing with people. Colourful stalls of fruits and vegetables, pots and pans, toys and trinkets, attracted shoppers looking for a bargain. Sharda Prasad, a teacher at the local school was visiting the market with his wife Ramdulari and their four-month-old boy. The teacher moved a bit away from his family to buy fruits. Suddenly a sharp cry could be heard above the commotion.

"Nanhe! my little one, Nanhe!" cried Ramdulari. She had tripped and fallen down.

Sharda Prasad rushed to his wife. "Are you alright? Where is Nanhe?"

"He rolled out of my arms when I fell. Someone picked him up. I thought it was you," cried his wife.

Sharda Prasad and Ramdulari began searching for their child frantically, asking everyone around if they had seen him. After searching for an hour, the father walked towards the riverbank. The rivers Ganga and Yamuna come together at Prayag to form a holy confluence, making it a bustling pilgrimage centre. Many ferry boats were moored near the steps of the ghat, ready to take passengers across the water. Just as he was about to give up, Sharda Prasad spotted a baby in a basket in one of the boats. He ran towards the boat, even as it was about to leave the jetty. He realised it was indeed his son. He picked him up with relief and exclaimed. "How did you get here my son? What a fright you gave your mother and me!"

A woman sitting next to the basket looked up. "Your son? Put him down, Bhaiya. He is mine. God has given him to me."

Sharda Prasad was upset. "How could that be? He is my son! Born to my wife!"

"Where is she? Call her here," said the woman.

Ramdulari was sent for. The moment she saw her baby, she burst out into happy tears and hugged the baby. "Ah, Nanhe! You are safe."

The baby cooed and giggled in his mother's arms. The woman was convinced that Ramdulari was indeed the baby's mother. The parents thanked the woman and rewarded her for taking care of the baby. The little boy was none other than Lal Bahadur Shastri. The second prime minister of India.

The boy was barely one and a half years old when his father passed away. He grew up in his grandfather's house at Mughalsarai, another town in U.P. and attended the local school. One day his mother was scolding him for breaking a glass, when his uncle came to his rescue. "Leave the child alone. Don't scold him. He is a fatherless boy."

"All of you pamper him too much," said Ramdulari shaking her head.

Nanhe was happy to get out of trouble. He grew mischievous by the day.

On the way to school, there was a private garden full of fruit-laden trees. Nanhe and his friends would eye the ripe fruits hungrily as they passed by. One day, they made a devious plan to jump over the high compound wall and steal the fruits.

"What fun! But I'm too short. You will have to help me over the wall," Nanhe told the boys.

The boys entered the garden, climbed the trees and feasted on the juicy fruits. Just then, they spotted the gardener coming towards them with a stick in his hands. The scared boys jumped over the wall and ran away. But little Lal Bahadur was not able to cross the wall by himself and was caught.

"Naught boy! How dare you steal from my garden," said the gardener smacking him.

"Why did you beat me? Don't you know, I don't have a father?" said Lal Bahadur in tears.

"That means you will have to look after your mother. How can a thief take care of anyone?" said the gardener.

Lal Bahadur was taken aback. He was so used to people fussing over him and letting him get away with mischief as they pitied him for being a fatherless boy. He had never given a thought to his responsibilities. "What you say is correct," he said, full of remorse. "I promise to be a good boy from now on."

Lal Bahadur spent more time studying and less time making mischief, after that. Ramdulari was happy to note the change that had come over her son. He was growing up to be a sincere and responsible boy.

When Lal Bahadur passed the sixth standard, he was sent to a school in Varanasi. The people he stayed with were not kind to him and would order him around. He would have to do the household chores in the mornings and then leave for school. He had to take the ferry to cross the river, as his school was on the opposite bank.

One morning, Lal Bahadur stood on the steps of the ghat, looking at the Ganga River flowing calmly below. The boatman had not allowed him on the ferry, as he did not have any money to pay him. After a moment's hesitation, he made up his mind. He tied his schoolbooks in a bundle and jumped into the river – Splash! The ice-cold water stung his skin. Holding the bundle above his head to avoid it from getting wet, Lal began to swim across the mighty river, with one hand. From then on whenever he didn't have enough money for the ferry, he would swim and make it to school on time.

One day his teacher Mishraji announced in

class, "Children, let's go to the fair. Have all of you brought the money?"

All the students put up their hands except one.

Mishraji went up to him. "Aren't you coming, Lal Bahadur?"

"Umm...no," said the boy unable to look up from his desk.

After school the teacher waited for Lal Bahadur and spoke to him kindly. When the little boy finally confessed the difficulties he had been facing, Mishraji was moved by his plight. He took him to his house.

"Bhabo, tell me how many sons do we have?" he asked his wife as she opened the door.

"Why, three... said his wife in surprise.

"Wrong. We have four sons now," said Mishraji with a hand on Lal Bahadur's shoulders.

From that day on, he became a member of the teacher's family. He finally found the love he had always yearned for. And it was here that the seeds of nationalism were sown into his young mind.

Lal Bahadur was fond of listening to stories told by Mishraji, about how India lost her freedom. "The British, who came to India as traders, stayed on to become our rulers. Naturally they are interested in trade and not in the welfare of our people."

"Sir, can't we do anything about it?" said Lal Bahadur.

"We must educate our people. We must tell them what their rights are. You must do it when you grow up," replied the teacher.

"I will! I must serve my country when I grow up," he resolved.

His resolve got a boost when Mahatma Gandhi came to Varanasi. A huge crowd had gathered to hear Gandhiji's speech. Young Lal Bahadur was one of them. Gandhiji's spoke about not tolerating the harsh treatment meted out by the British, not cooperating with them and building a new India. The fire of patriotism was ignited in Lal Bahadur. He began to take a keen interest in the political affairs of the country. He would gather his friends after school and they would discuss their ideas.

"Can we achieve Swarajya through non-cooperation?" asked his friend.

"Gandhiji believes we can," said Lal Bahadur.

"I think he is right. A government cannot function without the cooperation of the people," said another boy.

"And we won't cooperate with the government because it is not our government," said Lal Bahadur. "We will not pay taxes. We will boycott the courts..."

"What about the schools run with government aid? Will you boycott the classes?" they asked.

"That is a difficult decision to make," said Lal Bahadur thoughtfully. It was easier to talk about the principles in general but implementing them in real life would be much more difficult.

A few days later when he and his friends went to write their exams, a group of students were protesting outside. They were appealing to all the students to boycott the government aided school. Lal Bahadur did not write his exam and went back home.

Bhabo was angry. "What! You have come back without writing the exam. Poor Ramdulari is waiting for you to start earning and here you go and waste a year of school."

Mishraji tried to get him to change his mind. "Patriotism is all right my child, but you also have to think of your family. They depend on you."

"No Mishraji, I cannot retract the steps I have taken. I want to serve my country," said Lal Bahadur respectfully but firmly.

He expected his mother to have the same opinion as Mishraji. But she surprised him by saying, "I have faith in you my Nanhe. Do whatever you think is right."

"Oh, thank you Ma. I am so relieved," said Lal Bahadur.

All those close to him knew that he would never change his mind once it was made up, for behind his small frame was the firmness of a rock.

Lal Bahadur began to take an active part in the non-cooperation movement. Dressed in white kurta-pyjama, with a white Gandhi topi on his head, he would carry out picketing and anti-government rallies, shouting slogans of "Mahatma Gandhi ki jai" and "Inquilab Zindabad".

Once, he was arrested, along with other students for taking part in a banned

procession but was let off with a warning as it was his first arrest.

Sometime later he joined the Kashi Vidyapeetha, a university that was founded and managed entirely

by Indians. He also started working in a khadi shop in the city. He would work after college and the whole day on Sundays. In 1926, after four years at the Vidyapeetha, Lal Bahadur earned a degree of 'Shastri' in philosophy, topping the list of candidates. Thus, the name Shastri stuck as a part of his name.

He went to take his mother's blessings. "Ma, I want to be a social worker. I have decided to join the organisation, the Servants of People Society."

"You have chosen a difficult path. May God be with you," said his mother.

The Servants of People Society was founded by Lala Lajpat Rai, a prominent leader of the Independence movement, to enlist and train missionaries for the service of the motherland. Lal Bahadur enrolled himself as a life member of the society and began to work for the welfare of the Harijans.

Two years passed in this manner. One day, Lal Bahadur got a telegram from his mother asking him to come home. In those days, telegrams were sent only in the case of an emergency. A worried Lal Bahadur rushed home.

"Ma, how is your health? Are you okay?" he said upon seeing her.

His mother smiled. "I have never felt better. I am soon going to have a daughter-in-law."

"A daughter-in-law?" Lal Bahadur asked, perplexed.

"Yes. I have chosen a bride for you," replied his mother.

That's how Lal Bahadur came to marry Lalita Devi. They settled down in Allahabad, where Lal Bahadur took charge as the secretary of the district Congress committee. Even though his means were meagre, their house was open to all.

One evening he came home with a friend. "We have a guest for dinner," he told his wife.

Lalita Devi looked at the small quantity of food she had prepared for themselves. "All right. Let's not think of our dinner. We will serve the guest first," she replied cheerfully.

"I knew you would find a way," said Lal Bahadur proudly.

In 1929, Lal Bahadur attended the historic Lahore session of the Congress. He came home to Allahabad charged with renewed enthusiasm. "The Congress has declared Purna Swarajya: complete independence, as its goal. We must get ready for a long non-violent struggle," he told his wife.

He addressed several meetings urging people to follow the path of non-violence and non-cooperation. "Stop paying taxes. Do not cooperate with the government. Even if some actions of the British make you angry, don't turn violent. Remember the words of the Mahatma."

At this time, several workers were arrested and jailed. Lal Bahadur was rarely seen at home. It would be late evening by the time he returned. His mother and wife were worried and brought it up during dinner. "I hear the jails are full of the protestors," said Lalita Devi.

"Yes, but there is still room for me," replied Lal Bahadur. Then looking at his wife, he added, "I will feel very unhappy if you cry when I am arrested. You must face it with a smile." A few days later he was arrested. Lalita Devi, remembered his words and did not shed tears.

Lal Bahadur was released from jail seven months later. It was a happy reunion with his family in Ramnagar. His wife had given birth to their first child, Kusum. Later they had two more children, Hari and Suman.

By the mid-thirties, he had served several jail terms. Once when he was in jail, he received news that his son Hari was unwell. He approached the jail warden for permission to visit his child.

"We know you are anxious to see your son. We will release you for one week, but on one condition," said the warden.

"What is it?"

"You must give a written promise that you will not take part in any political activity during this period."

"I am sorry, I cannot do that," said Lal Bahadur. "It goes against my principles. I have vowed to fight for our freedom."

Aware of his upright nature, the warden released him without a written statement. Lal Bahadur stayed by his son's bedside for a week, but Hari's condition worsened. At the end of the week the warden came to take him back to jail.

"But my son is seriously ill," said a worried Lal Bahadur.

"We cannot extend the permission...unless you give us the written promise," said the warden.

But Lal Bahadur was not prepared to give such a promise. He went near his son, caressed his head with love, took a deep breath and walked out of the house.

After his release, Lal Bahadur attended the meeting of the All India Congress Committee in Bombay in 1942. The 'Quit India' resolution was passed; they demanded the immediate end of British rule. The British government responded by throwing leaders like Gandhi and Nehru in jail. Lal Bahadur and a few of his associates left Bombay for Allahabad. They got down from the train before it could reach the platform, as they suspected the police would be waiting to arrest them at the station. They proceeded to tour the villages in disguise, spreading Mahatma Gandhi's message of 'Do or Die — either free India or die in the attempt.'

"But we have no one to guide us. All the leaders are in jail," said a farmer.

"You are your own leader. Gandhiji says every Indian who wants freedom must be his own guide. Everyone has to make an effort in order to be independent," said Lal Bahadur who was dressed as a farmer himself.

A few days later, he was to address a meeting at the clock tower in Allahabad. A huge crowd had

gathered to hear him speak. But the police came to know about it and arrested him. He was taken to an unknown location.

Lalita Devi was worried sick about him. The family faced hard times. After many months of waiting, she received a letter from her husband saying he was in Naini jail in U.P. She had to wait for another eighteen months to get permission to meet him. The children were delighted to meet their father, but Lalita Devi was saddened to see how weak and thin he had become. She was allowed to visit her husband once a week, but she was running out of savings. She began to cut down on expenses.

"Children, today we will have Bhowri with salt," said Lalita Devi to her children. It was a simple dish of wheat flour cooked with salt. The children ate it up hungrily. Kusum's neighbourhood friend had also joined them that day. She went home and told her mother. "Ammi, in Kusum's house everyone likes Bhowri very much. They have it every day. I too had some."

The concerned neighbour visited Lalita Devi's house the next day. She noticed there were no lentils or vegetables in the kitchen. The children's clothes, too, had become very shabby. She resolved to help them.

Soon, a man arrived at Lalita Devi's doorsteps with bags full of groceries, and other household supplies. She was astonished to see the spread. "Why have you brought all these provisions here? I don't have any money to pay for all this," she said.

"Don't worry. It's all paid for by your neighbour," replied the man.

Lalita Devi rushed to the kind neighbour's house. "You shouldn't have done so much, behan. You must have spent a lot."

"Oh Lalita, this is nothing. Lal Bahadur is doing so much for our country. It's our duty to help you whenever the need arises."

Lalita Devi was moved by her kindness.

Finally, in 1946 Lal Bahadur was released from jail and in 1947 India gained her independence. He was appointed as the minister for police in Uttar Pradesh. In his new role, he had to visit various cities. One such visit was to Agra. As the train pulled into the station, he saw a strange sight. The railway platform was filled with many uniform clad policemen and congressmen dressed in white Gandhi topis.

He alighted from the train and inquired about a nearby police officer, "What is all this about? Is some dignitary coming here today?"

"Don't you know? The police minister sahib is coming by this very train. Everyone has gathered to receive him. No one can leave until the minister leaves. Don't block the way."

"Don't worry I won't trouble you," said Lal Bahadur not revealing his identity. He quietly stood on the side.

One of the Congress workers recognised him. "The man you were talking to is the police minister," he said.

The police officer did not believe him. "Come on! I would be a fool to believe you. A minister would have half a dozen men around him. He wouldn't be alone. Now, now, this is no time for joking."

Finally, a group of Congressmen walked up to the minister and welcome him with garlands.

"You troubled yourselves unnecessarily my friends. All of you need not have come here just to receive me," said a humble Lal Bahadur.

Lal Bahadur Shastri took on the post of the general secretary of the Congress on Jawaharlal Nehru's request. He organised the poll campaign for the party leading to victory in the first general elections. He served the country in various capacities, as the minister of railways, minister of communications and later as home minister. He rose through the ranks through his hard work and efficiency. He came to be considered prime minister Jawaharlal Nehru's go-to person. All through this he remained simple and unassuming, preferring to dress in a simple white kurta with a Gandhi cap.

On May 27, 1964, Pandit Nehru died and the country was suddenly left without a head of state. The Congress party met to elect its new leader. Lal Bahadur Shastri was late to the meeting. The party president K. Kamaraj had already started his speech, so he waited behind, near the steps.

"I propose the name of Shastriji as our new leader," Kamaraj announced.

Shastriji was surprised to hear his name. All the members agreed to the proposal and thus the mild-mannered and soft-spoken Lal Bahadur Shastri was appointed as India's second prime minister.

During his tenure, he introduced many measures to help the common man. His main

goal for the country was to have self-sufficiency in food. He promoted the Green Revolution in India leading to an increase in food grain production. He enabled fair-price shops to be set up in all parts of the country. The rising price of cloth was also controlled. Stern action was taken against black marketeers, smugglers and food-hoarders.

A year passed by. Then in 1965, Pakistan attacked India on the Kashmir front. "We will meet force with force. Jai Jawan, jai Kisan!" Shastriji announced. This slogan encouraged people to support the Indian armed forces and also recognised the important role that farmers play in the country's economy. His leadership during the war earned him widespread respect. People realised that the prime minister may look meek, but the little man could roar like a lion.

In January 1966, a cease-fire was brought about. Lal Bahadur Shastri left for Tashkent in Russia to hold talks with Ayub Khan, the president of Pakistan. Before his departure, he spoke about his intentions, "I can assure you, my countrymen that our nation's independence will not be compromised. I will press for peace—peace with honour."

In Russia, discussions were held between India and Pakistan with the help of the Soviet Premier Kosygin. An agreement was signed by both the parties.

But the tension and strain took its toll on Shastriji. At midnight Lalita Devi and her son Hari were awakened by a phone call from Tashkent informing that Shastriji had taken ill. Sometime later in the night, he passed away. India lost another illustrious son.

The Bharat Ratna award was conferred upon him posthumously.

Lal Bahadur Shastri was a visionary who was determined to build a new India. He took on every challenge with a cheerful smile and a humble heart. The honest and courageous prime minister will always remain a pride of India.